to neverlasting
by landon

Copyright © 2022 landon

All rights reserved.

No part of this publication may be reproduced, distributed, or transmitted in any form or by any means, including photocopying, recording, or other electronic or mechanical methods, or by any information storage and retrieval system without the prior written permission of the publisher, except in the case of very brief quotations embodied in critical reviews and certain other noncommercial uses permitted by copyright law.

paperback ISBN: 978-0-578-67550-3

eBook ISBN: 979-8-9871422-9-5

Library of Congress Number: applied for

Published by Georgia Poe Lit,
the poetry department at Winn Publications

GeorgiaPoeLit.com
WinnPublications.com

Cover design: justice moore

to neverlasting
by landon

to justice and to him.

to neverlasting

i think u and i fall into one of
my favorite tropes.
'right person, wrong time.'
it's a perfect combination of

romance
&
      heartbreak.

but i'm beginning to think that
our combinations were off because
 i felt one more than the other.

to neverlasting

i miss how u would play with my hair
when i laid my head on ur lap.
i miss our spiderman kisses and laying
in my bed late at night listening to that
one song by push baby.
i miss hearing ur voice over the phone
while we talked about anything until
four in the morning on a school night.
i just..
      i just miss
          y o u.

landon

i wish i had the chance to introduce
u to my parents.
they probably wouldn't have liked
u but it still would have been special
to do so.
because i've never liked as anyone as
much as i ~~do~~ did u.
and i don't think i will again.

to neverlasting

i'm sorry i snored,
    but i'm glad u remembered
    i did.

landon

i hate how i overthought absolutely everything in our relationship
and how i let myself sabotage the one good thing i had in my life.
we still talk and we're still friends but i don't want to be that with you.

to neverlasting

i have a belief that everyone gets to be selfish,
that u should be able to do whatever the fuck
u want no matter what people think or say.
    but in my case, i don't believe i have
    the right to be.

landon

thinking of u like this still is what will be

m
  y
              d
             o
                w
                   n
                      f
                     a
                       l
                         l.

maybe that's just what i get for being an idiot.

to neverlasting

sometimes i regret continuing to be friends after breaking up,
    but we only had each other in the end.

landon

i hate the way i ended things,
but i think i hate the way u handled things even more.

to neverlasting

you're with the person that told u to ask me out.
the person who was there with me whenever shit went down,
the same person who was first to know that i was going to break up with you.
the person who told me what i was thinking was not normal.

i hope you find that as amusing as i do.

landon

i wonder if there was any overlap between us
and ur new relationship.
                        it didn't take u long to
                        go   for   my   friend.

to neverlasting

i hope in a multiverse
i never told u how i felt.

landon

i see our relationship now like the weeds
that grow out of the concrete.

something that's broken the foundation
completely and can never be restored to
its originality.

to neverlasting

i apologize for everything.
i only have myself to blame for
this situation.

landon

i will always regret saying that u
only felt like a friend. because i
think i only said it to make myself
feel better.

to neverlasting

i don't want to remember
any of our conversations,
but of course they have to keep
me up at night when all i want
to do is go to sleep and forget.

landon

u make me want to go back into therapy.
but maybe writing all of this down is better.
at least it's cheaper anyhow.

to neverlasting

i remember the day after confessing, it sounds kind of childish to say it like that but i remember it vividly. the two of us walking up and down the street in the cold at ten o'clock under the barely visible stars in hopes that a restaurant was open so we could finally eat. i was trying to wrap myself in my thin gray jacket because i had decided that i wanted to wear a tank top that night since we were hanging out with our friends. i wanted to look nice, for u and for me. i remember wanting to hold your hand as we walked, wanting to feel the warmth of ur skin because even if it meant that the rest of my body had to be cold, at least i would be able to feel the heat radiating from ur hand onto mine. i remember walking back to their house, our food and my drink in our hands. we sat in front of the door because it was locked and we ate. u had shared some of ur food with me because they got it wrong and u didn't want to waste anything. we talked, we laughed. i was with you and everything was good, great in fact. it had been one of my favorite memories, but now it's beginning to be one of my worst.

landon

my love for you
is neverlasting.

to neverlasting

i wonder what u did with the stuff i gave u.
the bracelets, the stupid plastic rings i got
from the arcade, even the earrings i gave u
from my jewelry box.
i hope u kept them, but i know you probably
didn't

landon

u told me u love her,
and that was hard to hear.
but when u continued to say
that u were at ur breaking point
with her,
i nearly cheered.

to neverlasting

i should've trusted myself
more with u.

landon

"i thought about breaking up
             with him."
                         "i thought about breaking up
                                with her."
two different conversations,
two different people,
but just one toxic relationship.

to neverlasting

you said the day u two break up is the day you'll tell me everything,
but i don't think i can stay here waiting any longer.

landon

i wished i could've
kissed u more.

to neverlasting

i miss our movie nights and late night talks. i miss your laugh and the way you used to smile at me. i miss having my arms around your neck to pull you close and laying on your shoulder, our soft late night kisses as we laid on my bed. i miss having my head in your lap under the christmas lights that were hung on the walls of my room. i miss when you being a big part of my life. i miss you, i miss all of you, everything little thing about you. but missing you now makes me feel pathetic and utterly miserable.

landon

i still think about ur
eyes sometimes, how
they reminded me of
b l u e b e r r i e s.

but now i have to remind
myself that i never liked
blueberries.

to neverlasting

i just want to hate u,
but maybe it's easier
to make u hate me.

landon

i can't wait until you're
just a distant memory.

a thought that is completely forgotten.

to neverlasting

i lost the three people who were closest
to me last year, in the long run however,
it had been the best thing to happen to me.

and i have you to thank for that.

landon

thank u for making me feel wanted.
i can only hope i made u feel the same.

to neverlasting

i hope u wish me a happy birthday.
if u remember it.

landon

talking every day and night to
talking once a week with conversations
that usually ends with a fight.

to neverlasting

i think that i was willing to force u
into my own puzzle rather than try
to find the correct piece to complete it.

landon

her and i were so close.
now i'm just the ex.
nothing more, nothing less.

to neverlasting

i know i talk about our relationship like it lasted longer than it actually did, but i wish it had.
    i'm sorry about that.

landon

i hate love.
it blurs the lines and
fucks with ur head in
a way that can't be corrected.

to neverlasting

i don't know why i still think about this stuff,
it's been months.

seven months.

landon

i remember the happiness i felt when
u asked me to do ur eyeliner and paint
ur nails. the happiness that we both felt
in that moment.

to neverlasting

u make me feel so bitter,
i can almost taste it.

landon

maybe the day u and her break up,
we'll be okay.
but i don't think that's ever gonna happen.

to neverlasting

>i liked to look at my life through a camera lens.
at least then i could give myself a happy ending.
and if that happy ending ended with you,
so be it then.

landon

i wish that i could go back to my childhood.
back to when i didn't need to worry about how
all of my decisions would affect me.

to neverlasting

it took u less than three weeks to get with someone new.
but it's taken me seven months to finally say how i feel.

landon

in another life i hope that
we never fucking met. that
our paths never fucking corssed.

to neverlasting

as much as i hate u, i do love u.
i hope we're still friends by the end,
but that's not even a probability anymore.

landon

sometimes i wish u were still
my comfort person,
but i'm glad i have her now instead of u.

to neverlasting

every time u and her got into a fight
i couldn't help but think,
"god i hope they break up this time."

landon

today at a glance my horoscope said,
    "troubled relationships
        will make u feel
            troubled."
im beginning to think that even the universe
knows how shitty u truly make me feel now.

to neverlasting

the prospect of me still feeling for u
like that terrifies me.
           especially now that i can see
                u for who u really are.

landon

u told me that u hated fake people.
so, it begs the question:
    why are u still with her?

to neverlasting

i thought that once i graduated i would be happy.
but i also thought that i would still be friends with
those three or at least have you by my side.
                              i guess things just happen.

landon

i don't want to know how it's gonna feel
when you're gone completely from me.
but i think it's about time to start learning.

to neverlasting

i'm giving up my hope on u.
and that's probably been my
best decision yet.

landon

i hope u get that these poems are about u.
i also hope u feel like shit when u read them.

to neverlasting

i'm starting to think that maybe
i just don't know how to love properly.
i don't think i was ever really taught.

landon

i'm too young to know what
life, love, and loss feel like.
but maybe that i'm starting to
get the sense of all of it.

to neverlasting

we toast to everlasting love,
                but i clink my glass to neverlasting.

landon

i think there was a point in time where i was so content with
everything that i was willing to put my own feelings aside in
order to keep the same contentment that was felt in the moment.

to neverlasting

our realtionship was like my favorite
candle that burned out too
quickly for my liking.

landon

i like to think that i was better to you then,
than the way she is to you *now*.

to neverlasting

it baffles me that the only reason i found out about you two
was because we kissed.
and i think to myself, if that had never happened,
do you think you would have ever told me?

landon

i counted the days when
we broke up to when
i found out.
only three weeks.
to the day.

to neverlasting

i remember walking in on you two making out.
in my bedroom.
on my couch.

landon

i wish that i could just forget
e   v   e   r   y   t   h   i   n   g
about   you.

to neverlasting

you said my

s   e
 m i l

was your favorite thing
about me.
i wish it still was.

landon

i dreamt about our lives together.
christmas and late night talks in a
shared bed. it was something that i
had truly wanted with you.
but dreams are always short lived,
aren't they?

to neverlasting

the times i spent with you,
were my highest.
now they're my lowest.

landon

i wonder if you know that
she cheated on her ex.

twice.

to neverlasting

i learned that if i couldn't change my environment,
i needed to change myself instead.
i think that's why i'm doing better now.

landon

every single word i have ever said to you feels empty. like nothing i have ever said got through and it now all remains meaningless. just sitting inside your head hoping, trying, fighting to get any attention that it possibly can get so you can finally hear it. so you can finally put a meaning to the now empty word.

to neverlasting

to truly think about it,
we were always neverlasting.
our fate was sealed from the
beginning.

landon

my attachment is unhealthy as ever.

to neverlasting

i wish you were still the
only
    thing
keeping me going.

landon

our relationship evaporated
as quickly as candle wax.

to neverlasting

all i have now are the memories,
though i don't know if those are
enough for me anymore.

landon

you feel like my nicotine addiction.
the only difference is that i'm five
months free of nicotine and i don't
think about it anymore.

to neverlasting

i'm starting to regret all my tears
that revolved around you.
what a waste.

landon

with you, i entered uncharted waters.
and i drowned within seconds.

to neverlasting

12,00 dreams were interpreted.
and now none of them involve you..

landon

you liked my short hair,
so now i'm starting to
grow it out.

to neverlasting

you're never going to come back to me,
are you?

landon

i used to look at her in resentment, thinking
that that should have been me next to you,
though now im beginning to be glad that i'm not.

to neverlasting

the thought of you is beginning to ruin my life.

landon

if i could do this all over,
i'd do all of this differently.
that way i didn't need to be
in my current state.

to neverlasting

i'm finally going to delete your number.
i don't have any more use for it, do i?

landon

you remind me now of the pain and inconvenience
you have when you bite your tongue.

to neverlasting

i wish i could forget everything i know about you, it's
    useless
           to me now.

landon

the ghost of you will always
be better than the real you.

to neverlasting

i don't think i know who you are anymore,
but that's a good thing isn't it?

landon

you feel so suffocating to me now,
like you've putten a bag over my head
in hopes you can kill me.

to neverlasting

you never really understand how
truly good you have it until you
finally   lose   it.

landon

the more i think of you,
the angrier i begin to feel.

to neverlasting

if you ever read this, and i hope you do, i need you to understand.
i need you to understand that you make me so undeniably angry now
that it is insane. that every thought i have of you now in this point of
time makes me sick to my stomach. that now i will never be able to look
at you and her the same way that i used to be able to. that the only feeling
that fuels me now is some sort of hatred.

landon

the thought of you with her is beginning to tear up my insides.
tearing through my organs piece by piece. veins and vessels
being pulled apart one by one, my heart strings being torn out
so slowly it makes me want to scream.

to neverlasting

as much as i am beginning to hate you,
i understand that it's all my fault for the
way i feel.
but i couldn't just go back to you, it didn't
feel fair, but now i do think that i should've.

landon

your lips tasted like mint.
cold and a little hard to get
used to.

to neverlasting

i wanted my lips to travel all around you,
to kiss every individual part of you and
to have it all feel truly loved.

landon

i thought i knew what i wanted
when i ended things, but it's
obvious now that i didn't.

to neverlasting

people my age romanticize the idea of love and heartbreak so much. it's like they really want to feel the hateful pain that engulfs you and hits you straight in your chest. it burns like a wildfire that no one's able to put out. like there's a knife stabbing you in the heart repeatedly, over and over and over again. like all of your organs are beginning to fail one by one and you're slowly dying inside day by day.

landon

no matter how hard i try to keep you away from the back of my head,
you keep coming back.
but at least every time you do, you come back weaker than before. you
come with the fight to stay but each time it's never enough, so you continue
to get beat and fought out. you continue to get weaker and weaker,
and you continue to get easier to forget about.

Made in the USA
Columbia, SC
16 October 2022

69449570R00065